How Pirates Really Work!

Yo-ho-ho
and a nice
cup of tea

Sea Monsters

Greenland

North America

North Atlantic Ocean

South America

South Pacific Ocean

South Atlantic Ocean

KEY

1. Sawfish
2. Sea Serpent
3. Neptune
4. Flying Fish
5. Hippocampus
6. Hydra
7. Medieval Monster
8. Sea Worm
9. Charybdis
10. Mermaid
11. Sea Unicorn
12. Tree Fish
13. Island Fish
14. Sea Cow
15. Indian Mermaid
16. Elephant Fish
17. Rainbow Fish
18. Giant Octopus
19. Cetus
20. Sea Lion
21. Sea Wolf
22. Sea Bishop
23. Sea Dog
24. Umibõzu
25. Godzilla
26. Giant Catfish
27. Sea Serpent
28. Bunyip
29. Makara
30. Equator Worm
31. Siren

Greenwich Meridian (0 degrees)

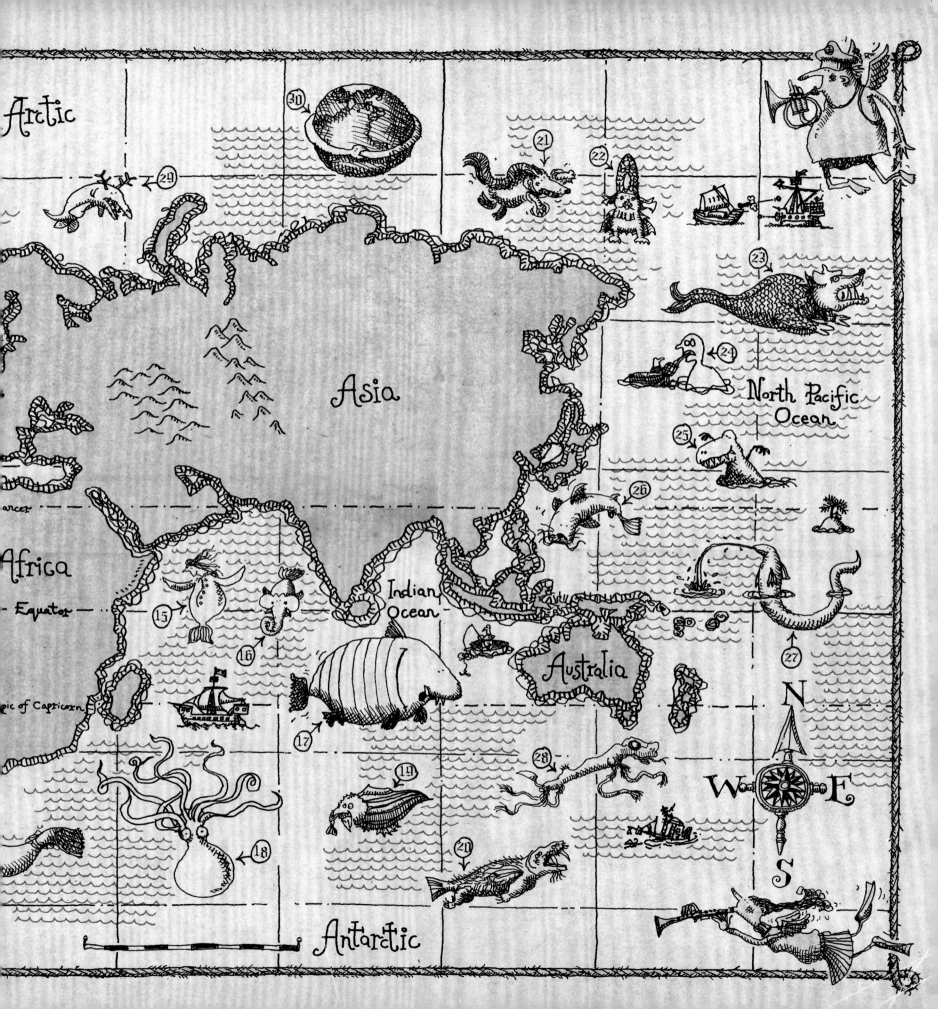

To Black Hearted Jaine,
Bosun Finn, Naughty Nell,
South-sea Caitlin the Cat, Rock Salt
Thomas, Fast Dagger Freddie, Red Inigo,
Scurvy Hal, Camille the Mermaid of the
Seine, Barrel Chucker Finn, Adam
Rackham, Javier the Spaniard & Izzy
& her performing seahorses

Published in Great Britain in 2013
by Simon and Schuster UK Ltd
1st Floor, 222 Gray's Inn Road, London, WC1X 8HB
A CBS Company
Text and illustrations copyright © 2013 Alan Snow
The right of Alan Snow to be identified as the author and illustrator
of this work has been asserted by him in accordance with the
Copyright, Designs and Patents Act, 1988
A CIP catalogue record for this book
is available from the British Library upon request
Printed in China
1 3 5 7 9 10 8 6 4 2

ISBN: 978 0 85707 955 8 (HB)
ISBN: 978 0 85707 956 5 (PB)
ISBN: 978 0 85707 957 2 (eBook)

How Pirates Really Work!

by Alan Snow

SIMON AND SCHUSTER

London   New York   Sydney   Toronto   New Delhi

And So My Story Begins...

It all began some threescore years ago in a small town in the West. I lived with my mother and twenty-six brothers and sisters in a tiny cottage. There was always a lot happening in our busy little town and I would spend all my time down at the harbour watching what went on. I never grew tired of seeing the fishing boats and merchant ships come and go with all their varied cargoes.

The sailors sang hearty songs and would sometimes throw a small part of the day's catch or some other titbit my way. I always wondered what it might be like to live out on the open seas, rolling in the deep.
One night, I noticed a ship arrive very quietly. I watched as the crew tied up and made their way to the pub. I crept along behind them. After seeing how jolly they were, I decided to stow away and go to sea with them.

Setting Sail

I hid below deck between two cannons, thinking that the crew wouldn't be using those at so early a stage of the journey. Soon I felt the ship begin to roll and dip and realised we had left the harbour. We were off!

I poked my head out from my hiding place and heard a shout of, 'Brazil! Look out! The best crew that ever there was is coming your way!' Brazil. I had heard the men speaking of it at the docks and knew that meant we sailed in search of gold. The ultimate booty! I could not have been more excited.

It wasn't long before I was discovered by the crew. At first they were angry, but they soon found plenty of use for me. First task: get to know the ship from top to bottom.

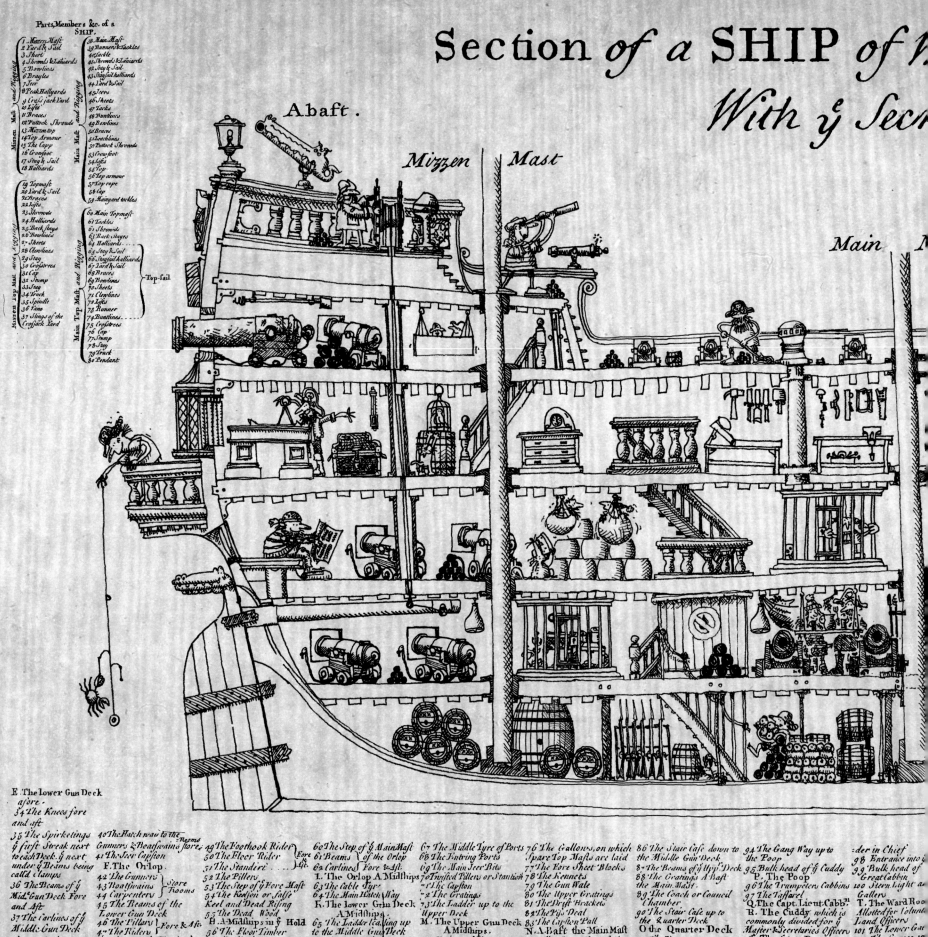

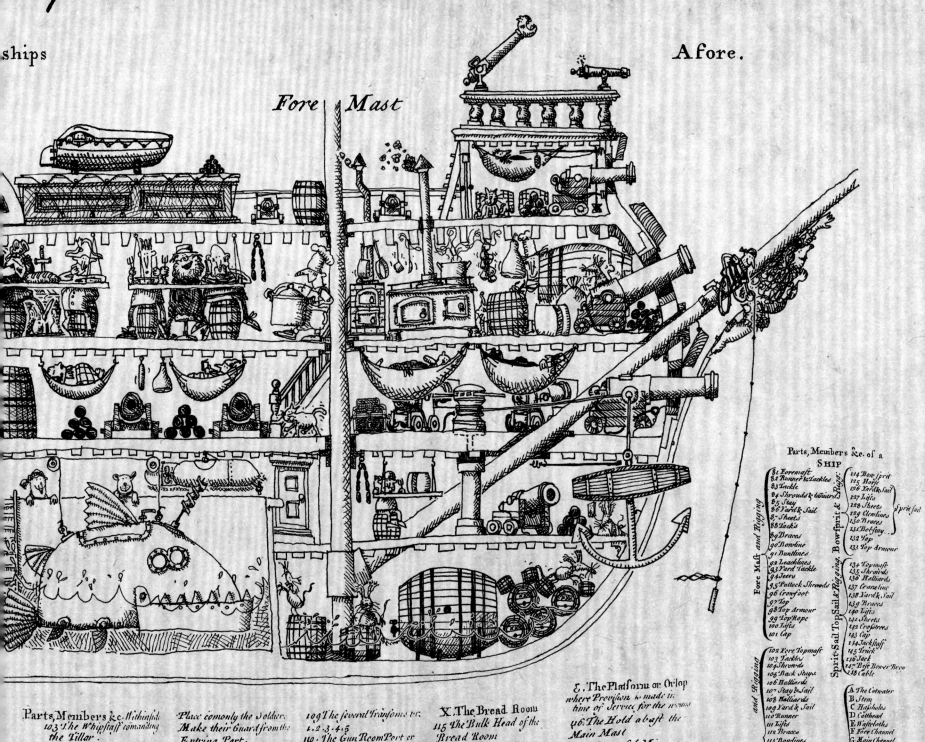

A DAY IN THE LIFE OF A PIRATE

The time on a ship is divided into four hour 'watches'. Sailors have to work a pattern of four hours on, four hours off. This goes right through the night.

1. GET UP AT 7 AM

2. WASH AND DRESS

5. LOOKOUT DUTY FROM CROW'S NEST

6. BREAK FOR SHIP'S BISCUITS
Break teeth, more like!

7. PRACTISE BALANCING 15 MEN ON A DEAD MAN'S CHEST

10. MORE SWABBING THE DECKS

11. LUNCH

14. CANNON PRACTICE

15. SINGING PRACTICE

Pirate Skills!

There are lots of things a trainee pirate needs to learn. It's a long way from Dorset to Brazil, so you get plenty of chance to brush up your new skills.

If we use a magnet we can make North any way we want!

NAVIGATION

First you have to learn to use a compass and a map, then work out the speed of the boat. There is an instrument called a sextant that's used to measure the height of the sun, and knowing this and the exact time, helps to work out where you are.

This is a sextant. Be very careful not to poke it in your eye or look directly into the sun.

SINGING. A good skill for all pirates. When we work together we might have to keep in time and at other times it helps keep us jolly.

Row, row, row your boat gently down the stream . . .

BOAT HANDLING. Without lots of practice it's almost impossible to sail a boat. But once you know how to, it can really help. Not only in everyday sailing but also when you are in a battle and need to use tactics.

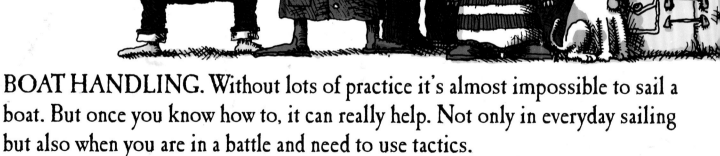

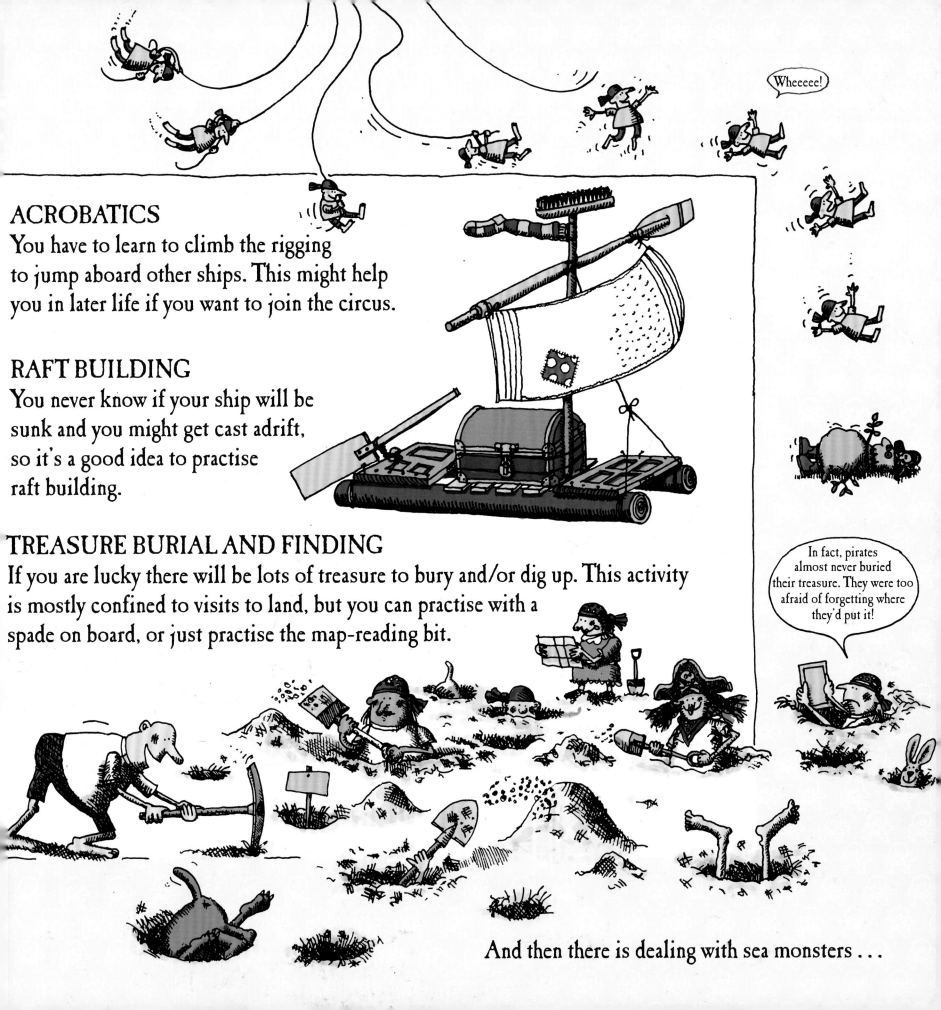

Wheeeee!

ACROBATICS

You have to learn to climb the rigging
to jump aboard other ships. This might help
you in later life if you want to join the circus.

RAFT BUILDING

You never know if your ship will be
sunk and you might get cast adrift,
so it's a good idea to practise
raft building.

TREASURE BURIAL AND FINDING

If you are lucky there will be lots of treasure to bury and/or dig up. This activity
is mostly confined to visits to land, but you can practise with a
spade on board, or just practise the map-reading bit.

In fact, pirates
almost never buried
their treasure. They were too
afraid of forgetting where
they'd put it!

And then there is dealing with sea monsters . . .

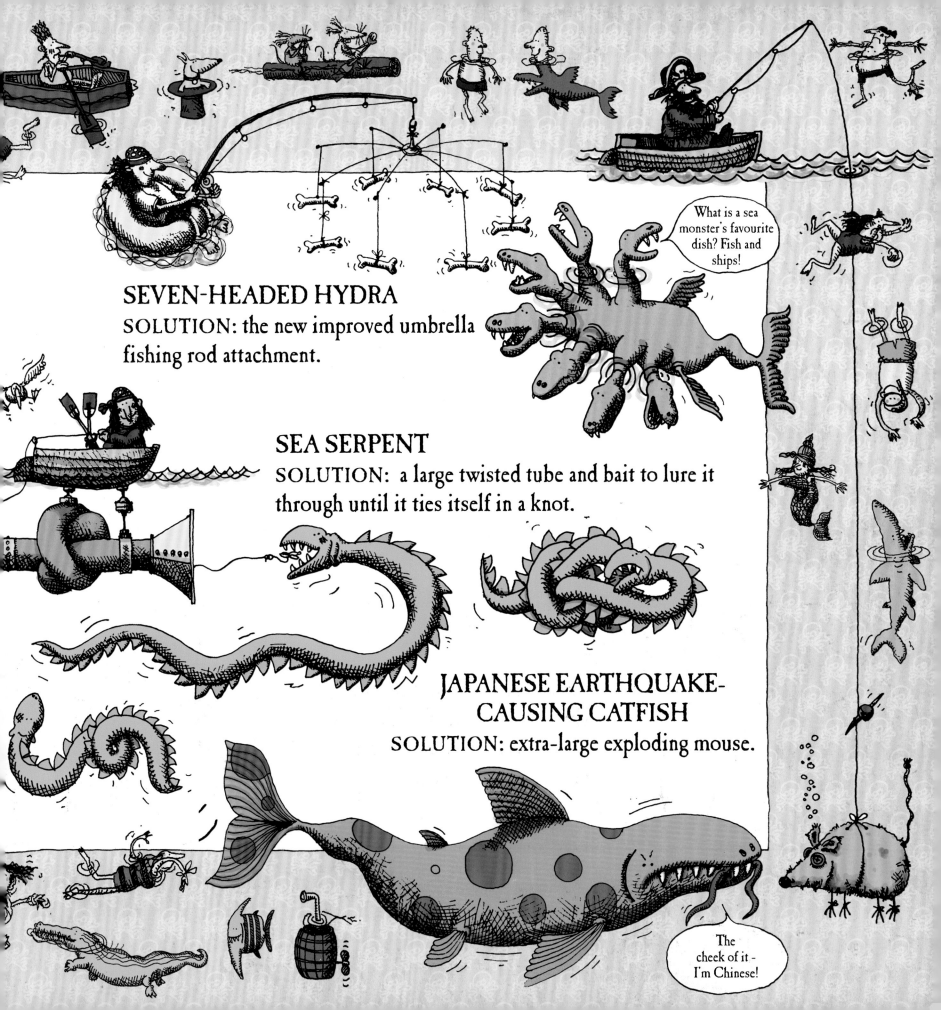

PARROTS!

People think pirates all have parrots. We don't! We hate parrots. They bite, talk and give away where you hide treasure and keep you up at all times of day and night with their squawking. Not only that but they get washed overboard. As we are expected to have parrots we have to have a way around this, and the answer is DIY parrots and a little bit of ventriloquism. What's more if you use a hook to act as a hand, you can operate the parrot and no one will guess.

HOW TO MAKE A PIRATE PARROT

1. Use three old socks, one for the body and head, and the other two for wings.

2. Use buttons for eyes but do try to find evil buttons to give the right effect.

3. A beak can be made of cardboard. This should be painted in a bright colour with waterproof paint as it is likely to get wet in storms.

4. You then have to learn ventriloquism (talking without moving your lips). False beards are useful for this.

What is orange and sounds like a parrot?

A carrot.

GROG + GRUB

If you like your food, you're in for a rough time at sea. Stored food goes off and even the water goes foul. After the first few weeks the only safe foods left are things that can be pickled, dried or preserved. If you're very lucky there might be fresh meat, eggs and milk from animals kept on board. Everything else goes rotten and mouldy. It's not healthy and lots of pirates got a disease called scurvy before it was discovered that lemons or pickled cabbage would stop you getting sick and all your teeth falling out.

Ship's biscuits are so hard you could use them to knock in nails! They are called 'hardtack' and are part of every meal, worse luck. We soak them to make them softer, but even then they are usually still wriggling with worms. Yuck!

A real treat is turtles and giant tortoises. They are really scrummy. (Although the shell is a bit too crunchy for my taste.) Dodos are also good to eat. A bit too good, unfortunately, and now they are all extinct!

Why are pirates the best?

Because they arrrrrr!

Treasure & Booty!

So you have got some treasure (or booty as it's known). What do you do with it?

Someone could come and steal it from you so it's best to hide it so only you and your crew can find it. The best thing is to bury it on an island where no one lives (that is why you did all the digging practice!) But you also have to make a map so you can find it again. But just in case the map falls into the wrong hands, it's best to use a code or clever clues to tell you where the treasure is buried so only you will know where it is. (In fact only one pirate, William Kidd, is known to have buried his booty.)

Many people think that we pirates are only interested in gold and silver in big wooden chests. And we do love all that, who wouldn't?

But there are plenty of other kinds of treasure that we value too. You might be surprised to discover that tea is very precious to us. We can do a roaring trade in the makings of a good cuppa so if we spot a ship coming home from China or India then we'll set our sights on it quick-sharp. And if you like a spoonful of sugar in your brew, then so do we, and any ships carrying sugar back from the Caribbean can expect a little visit from us too!

We are also always very glad to get our hands on cotton, spices, soap and even frying pans. We're not fussy!

What do you call a pirate who has lost his spade? Douglas.

What do you call a pirate with a spade? Doug.

Equipment & Weapons

Fearsome weapons for fearless pirates.

The cannon is the common name for this type of weapon, but each size used to have its own name.

POLE CANNON

SWIVEL GUN

DRAGON GUN

CANNONADE

LONG GUN

MORTAR

Even though we pirates are very brave, we do all we can to avoid actual fighting and instead like to put on a show to scare our enemies. If it does come to a fight, we use clever tactics so we don't damage the ships we want to take over.

THE CANNON

Botefeux

Cannonball

Rammer

Touch hole

Cannons were thicker and stronger where the explosion took place and thinner at the end of the barrel.

Charge

Wad screw

GUNPOWDER CHARGE
A fast and safe way to handle gunpowder. The charges were stored the magazine deep in the ship and brought up to the gun deck when needed.

We do use cannonballs, but also use different types of shot that damage an enemy ship but don't sink it.

CANNONBALLS
Good for sinking ships, and stored in racks or stands called brass monkeys.

CHAIN SHOT AND BAR SHOT
Take down sails and rigging.

CANNON GRENADES
Exploding bombs shot from the cannon.

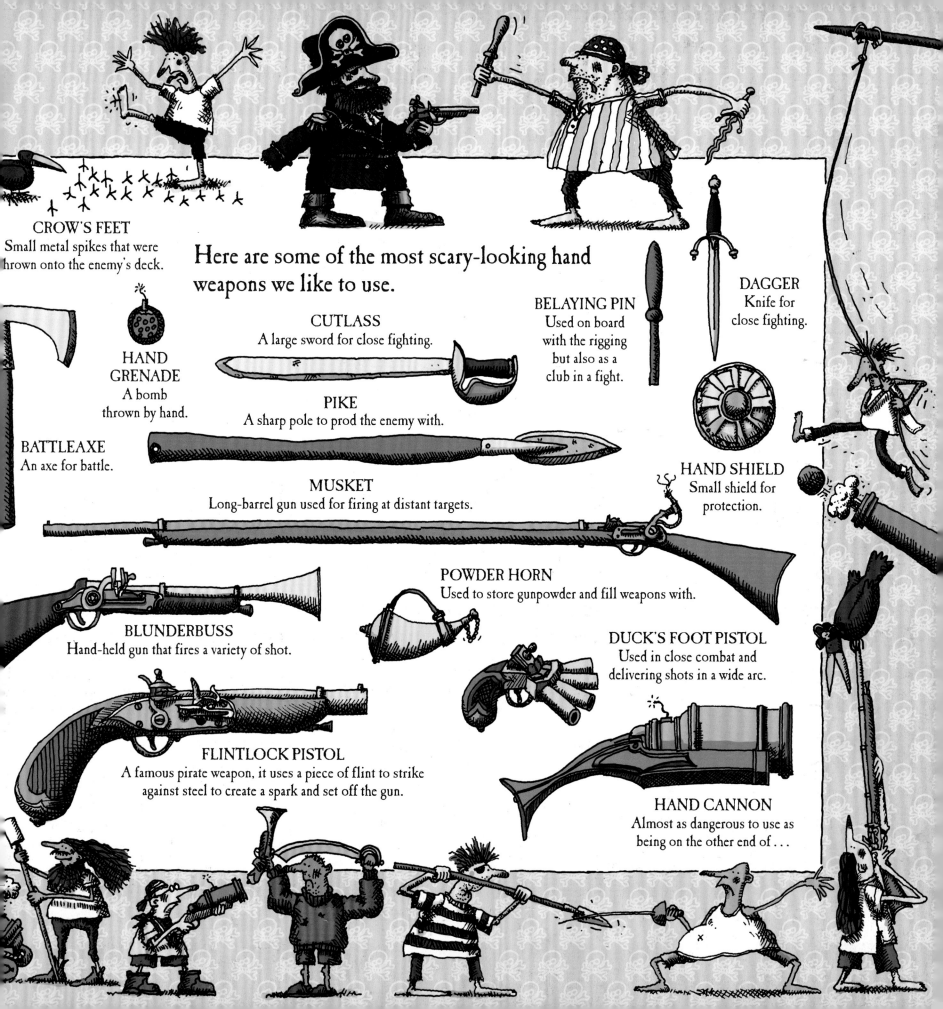

CROW'S FEET
Small metal spikes that were thrown onto the enemy's deck.

Here are some of the most scary-looking hand weapons we like to use.

HAND GRENADE
A bomb thrown by hand.

BATTLEAXE
An axe for battle.

CUTLASS
A large sword for close fighting.

PIKE
A sharp pole to prod the enemy with.

MUSKET
Long-barrel gun used for firing at distant targets.

BELAYING PIN
Used on board with the rigging but also as a club in a fight.

DAGGER
Knife for close fighting.

HAND SHIELD
Small shield for protection.

POWDER HORN
Used to store gunpowder and fill weapons with.

BLUNDERBUSS
Hand-held gun that fires a variety of shot.

DUCK'S FOOT PISTOL
Used in close combat and delivering shots in a wide arc.

FLINTLOCK PISTOL
A famous pirate weapon, it uses a piece of flint to strike against steel to create a spark and set off the gun.

HAND CANNON
Almost as dangerous to use as being on the other end of . . .

FAMOUS PIRATES

Ching Shih, a woman and one of the most successful pirates of all time, had a short career, taking early retirement when the government offered her the chance of an amnesty. She was undefeated by the British, Portuguese and Chinese and had a fleet of as many as 1500 ships.

Bartholomew Roberts was a very successful Welsh pirate who 'worked' the Caribbean. He had rules on his ships. For example, each man shall have equal vote, food and drink. Lights out at 8pm and no music on Sundays.

Blackbeard's real name was William Teach. He was famous for wearing flaming tapers in his beard. He died in a fierce battle with a force of Americans, sent to hunt him down.

Ann Bonnie married Calico Jack Rackham while on board his ship. She would fight and take on other duties as much as any other crew member. She and her husband were captured. Her husband was hanged, but she disappeared – some think her father paid a ransom to have her freed.

Captain Hook was a fictional pirate, and appears in Peter Pan by J M Barrie. He lost his hand to Peter Pan, which was then eaten by a crocodile! The crocodile went on to eat a clock.

Clock Eaten by Crocodile

Capt. Morgan

Captain Henry Morgan was a Welsh pirate who spent a lot of his time in the West Indies. He was given missions by the Governor of Jamaica to attack the Spanish and Dutch in the area. These missions were to gain riches for himself and the Governor, using the excuse of protecting Jamaica and the British interest. He probably died of a mix of too much drink and 'the dropsy'.

Jacquette Delahaye was a woman pirate from Haiti. She sailed the seas and robbed many but when she found herself too famous, she faked her own death and lived as a man for many years. When she returned as herself, she became known as 'Back from the Dead Red' because she had red hair.

What's the difference between Pirates, Privateers, & Buccaneers?

Pirates acted on their own, while Privateers acted with the agreement of at least one government. A group of outlaw pirates survived in the West Indies by cooking wild pig on sticks (buccan) and this is how they became known as buccaneers.

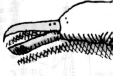

Barbarossa (Red Beard) was Turkish and an admiral of the Ottoman navy. He was very fierce and took control of the western Mediterranean while attacking the Spanish. He captured Algeria and made himself ruler, before handing it as a prize to the Ottoman emperor, who in return gave him two jewel encrusted swords.

Jack 'Calico' Rackham was an English pirate who was famous for pirating in the West Indies and also for designing his 'Jolly Roger' flag. This was a skull and crossed swords. He was eventually captured by the pirate hunter, Jonathan Barnet, in Jamaica. Rackham and most of his crew were hanged.

Captain Kidd was a Scotsman and not so much a pirate as a privateer and pirate hunter. He captured a number of pirate ships and in doing so made himself very unpopular with the East India Company, whose goods were often those he gained. He was hanged as a pirate in London after a trial which some say was a 'fix' involving the East India Company.

Long John Silver was a fictional pirate from Treasure Island. With his one leg and parrot on his shoulder, he is probably the most famous pirate of all. The typical 'pirate voice' (oooh arrgh) was based on the performance of the actor Robert Newton, who played Long John Silver in a movie.

Lady Mary Killigrew was an English 'lady' from Cornwall. She was said to have robbed a Spanish ship while it was in port and its officers were her guests. When they discovered their loss, the officers went to London to complain. Lady Killigrew was given a pardon when her son, a judge, 'interfered' with the investigation.

Charlotte de Berry was first recorded in a 'Penny Dreadful' magazine in 1836. It was said she disguised herself as a male pirate so she could travel with her husband, but he was killed and she was made to marry an officer who she hated and later killed. She was then captured by a captain, who took her as a wife but she killed him too and took his ship. Apparently.

Pirate Bling

Shark's teeth

Rings - bling, bling!

On board ship we wear simple clothes and shoes. But get us on land and it's a different story! We love to show off our fancy clothes. There's no point doing all that swashbuckling (theft some people call it) if we can't look good!

Hats are often part of a pirate's best outfits. We 'collect' them on our voyages, ahem.

We like to wear seashells as decorations.

Wearing bright colours used to be against the law - imagine that! Which is exactly why we like to wear them. We often steal rich fabrics and spicy perfumes from merchant ships. Hah!
So much for the rules.

Sometimes we do embroidery to fancy up our clothes.

Buckles

Walrus tooth scrimshaw

Silver breastplate

Stolen crucifix

African trading beads

Gold doubloon

Ostrich feath[ers] make splend[id] decoration[s] for hats.

THE MEANING OF PIRATE TATTOOS

a swallow for always returning home

an anchor shows an Atlantic crossing

a nautical star is for protection and guidance

a sparrow is for 5000 miles travelled

a rope around the wrist is to show a deckhand

a turtle for crossing the Equator

ship's lamps for Port (left side) and Starboard (right side)

a ship in full sail shows a trip around Cape Horn

the rooster and pig bring safety, ham, eggs and luck in a fight

EARRING[S]
1. Stop seasicknes[s]
2. Store wa[x] plug ears du[ring] cannon fi[re]
3. Can be us[ed] pay for a pir[ate] funeral

This Yap sto[ne] money is ju[st] too heavy

We pirates like to wear coins and other types of money as well as souvenirs from our voyages as part of our best outfits.

And that's about as much as I can tell you. I have sailed the seven seas, been marooned on a desert island, fought battles, won treasures, buried chests of gold – and now I'm sailing home to retire. It's been a rum old life, from stowaway to Pirate Captain. Which reminds me. Did I tell you my name?

It's **Captain Firebeard**.

At your service.

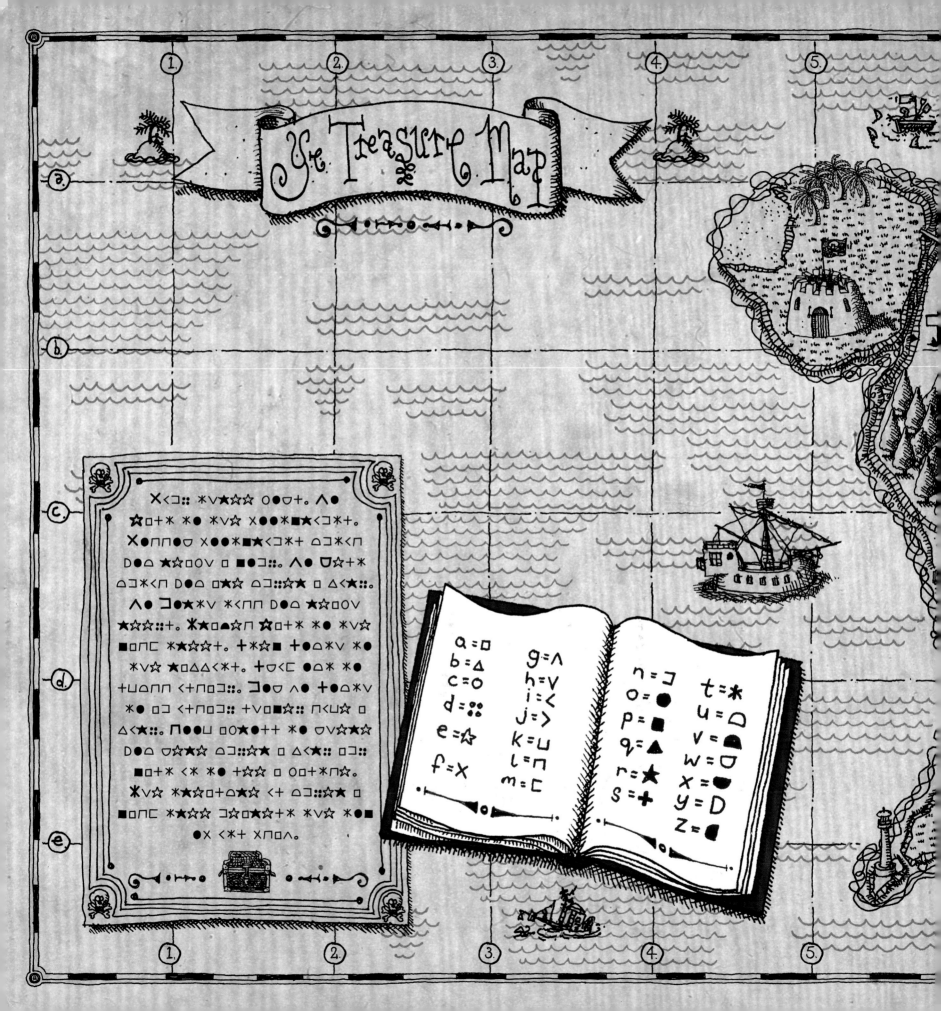

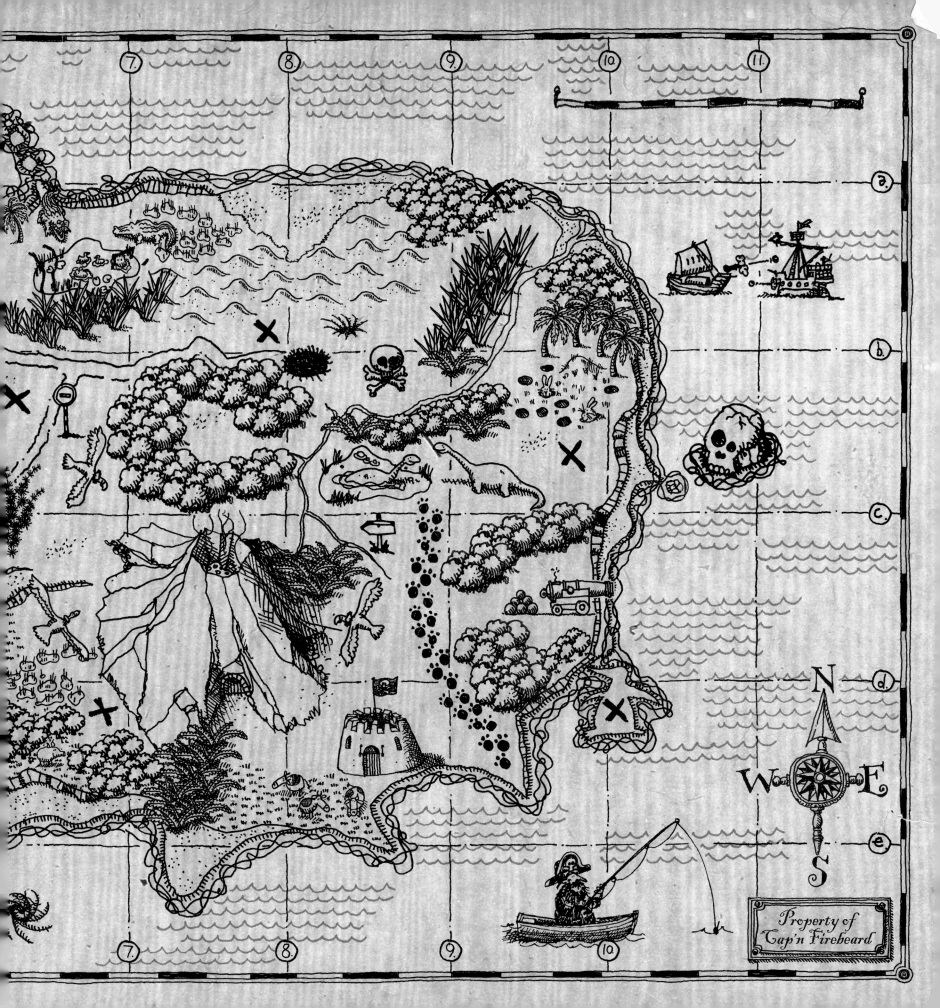

Property of
Cap'n Firebeard